A Little Princess Story

I Want A Friend!

Tony Ross

Andersen Press

"He doesn't want to play with me!"
wailed the Little Princess.

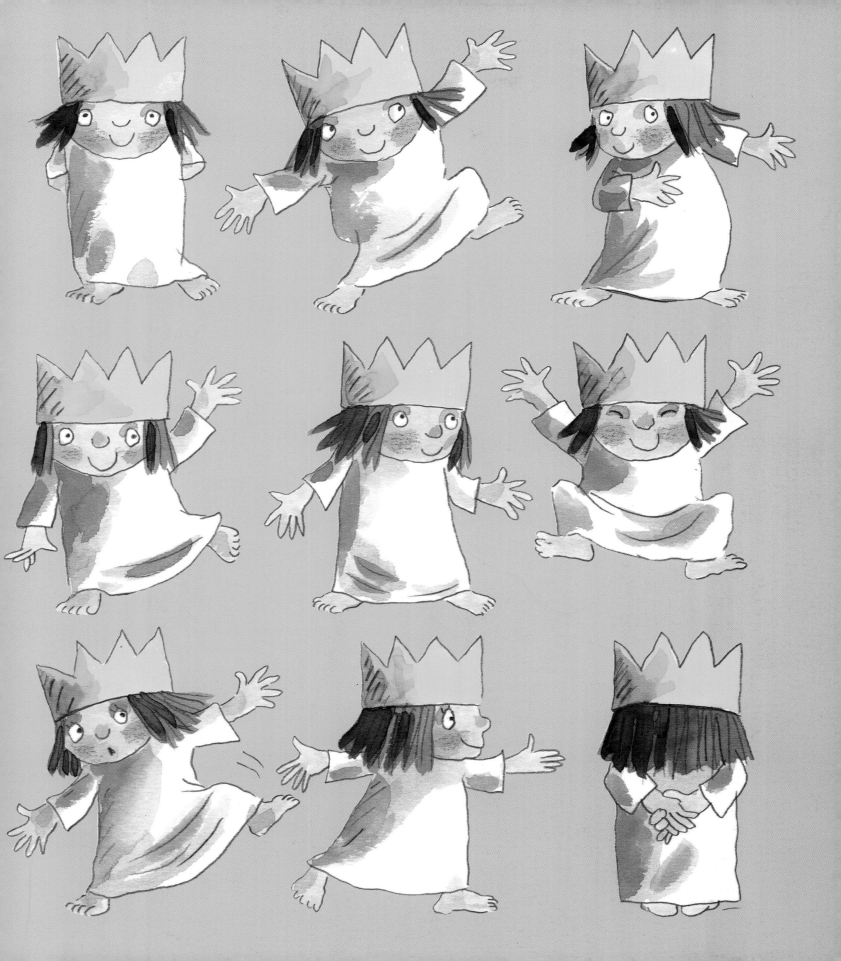

First published in Great Britain in 2005 by
Andersen Press Ltd., 20 Vauxhall Bridge Road, London SW1V 2SA.
This paperback edition first published in 2016 by Andersen Press Ltd.
Copyright © Tony Ross, 2005.
The rights of Tony Ross to be identified as the author and illustrator of this work
have been asserted by him in accordance with the Copyright, Designs and Patents Act, 1988.
All rights reserved. Colour separated in Switzerland by Photolitho AG, Zürich.
Printed and bound in Serbia.

3   5   7   9   10   8   6   4   2

British Library Cataloguing in Publication Data available.

ISBN 978 1 84939 285 3

This Little Princess

story belongs to

· · · · · · · · · · · · · · · · ·

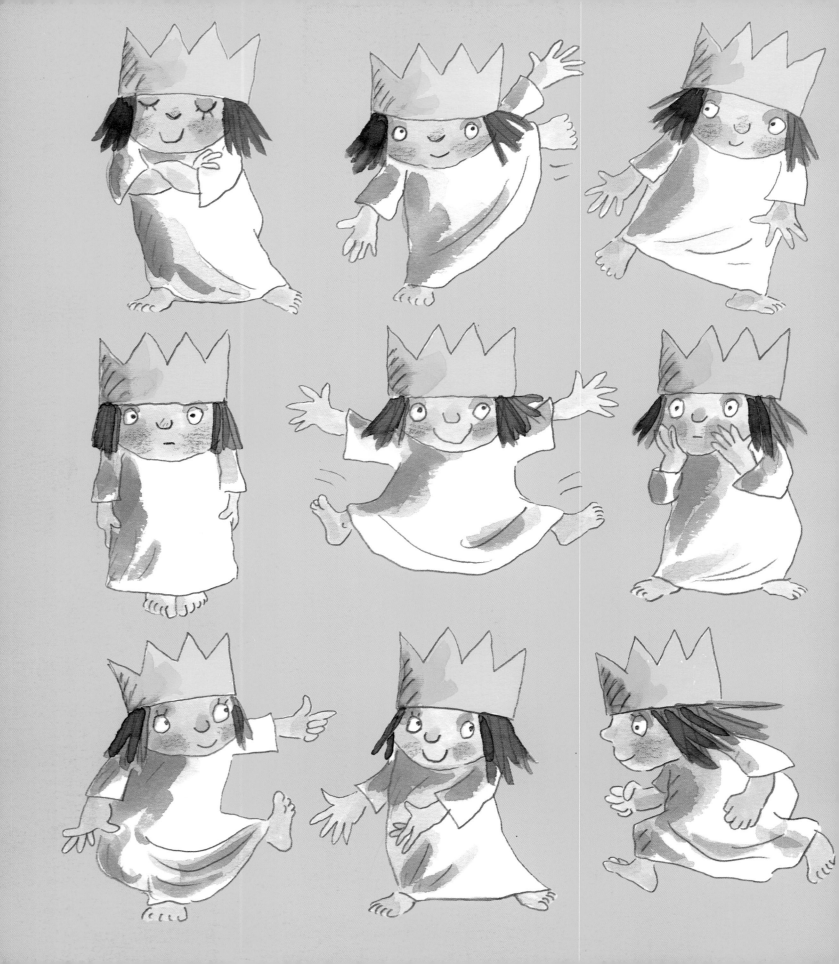

"He only does boys' stuff."

"Never mind," said the Queen. "You start school tomorrow. You'll have lots of friends to play with there."

Next day, at school, the Little Princess put
her hat and coat on her peg…

... and went to play with the other children.

Molly and Polly were skipping.
"We don't want to play with YOU," they said.

When Agnes came along, the Little Princess smiled.
"I don't want to play with YOU!" said Agnes.

"Can I play with you?" asked the Little Princess.
"No!" said Willy, and he went to play with Molly,
Polly and Agnes.

The Little Princess stood sadly by herself.
Then she saw another new girl standing by herself.

"Nobody will play with me," said the Little Princess.
"Nor with me," said the other girl.

There were lots of children standing by themselves.
"Nobody will play with us," said the Little Princess.
"Or us!!" said the lots of children.

The Little Princess and all the other children with no friends
shared their sweets and fruit.
"I wish I had a friend," they all said.

They all played tag together.
"It would be more fun if we had some friends," they all said.

In the classroom, all the children with no friends sat together.
Some other children with no friends joined in.

"Don't worry about having no friends," said the Little Princess
to the other new girl. "I haven't got any either. It's not so bad."
"It's not so bad," said all the others.

At going-home time, all the children with no friends helped each other with their coats and hats.

When the Little Princess put on her hat, Molly, Polly, Agnes and Willy gasped: "GOSH, SHE'S A PRINCESS!"

The Little Princess turned to all the other children with
no friends. "Would you like to come home to tea?" she said.

"Yes, please," they said.
"Can we come, too?" said Molly, Polly, Agnes and Willy.

The Little Princess frowned her terrible frown.

"All right," she said. "Come on."

"Goodness!" said the Queen. "Who are all these children?"

"My friends," said the Little Princess.

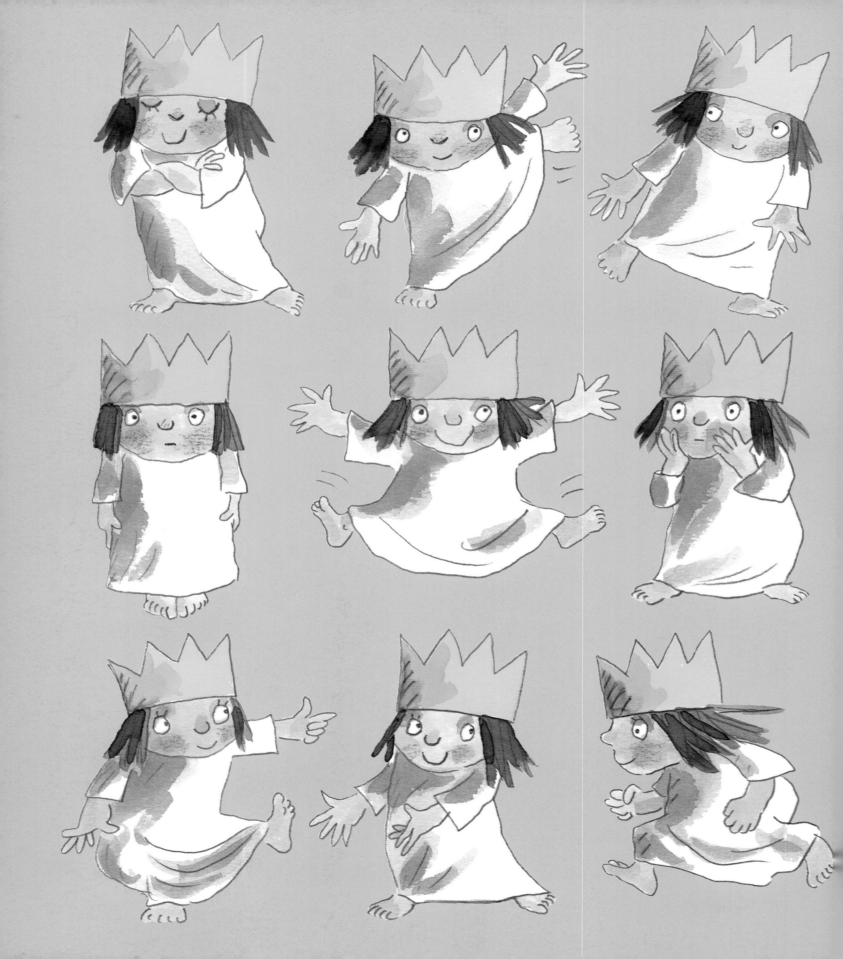

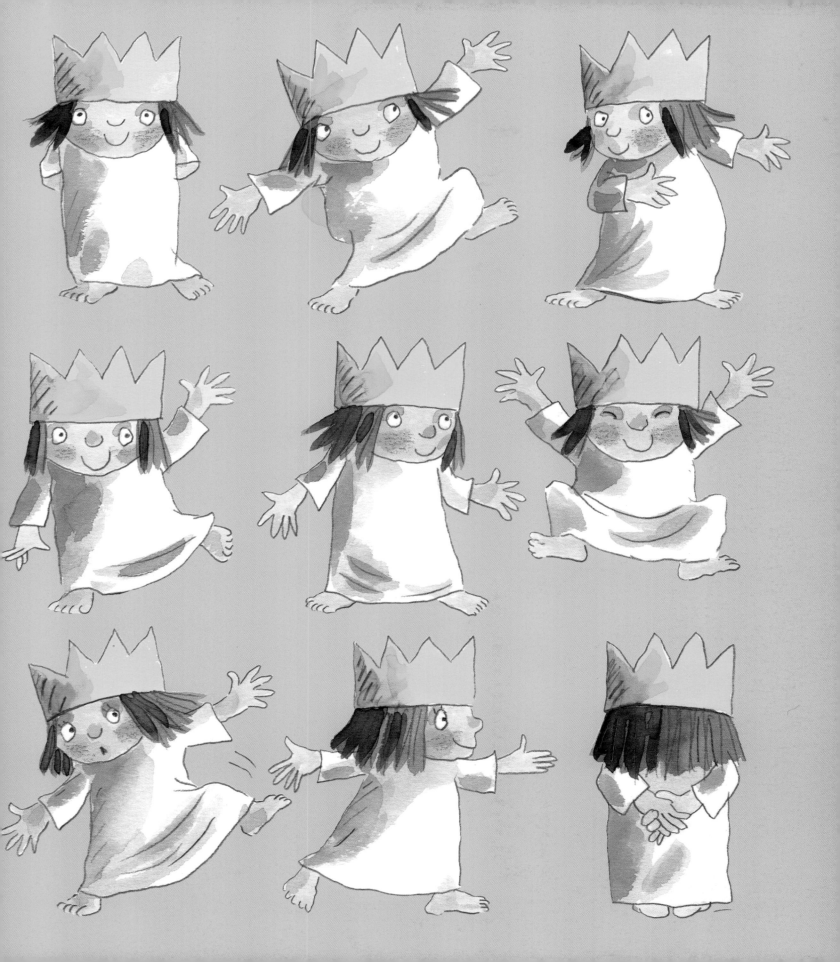